PARMO

to the
Rescue!

**Written by Rachael Wong and inspired
by the children of Middlesbrough**

Illustrated by children from across the town

BREWIN BOOKS

First published by
Brewin Books Ltd, 19 Enfield Ind. Estate,
Redditch, Worcestershire B97 6BY in 2020

www.brewinbooks.com

ISBN: 978-1-85858-720-2

A Cataloguing in Publication Record
for this title is available from the British Library.

Typeset in Calibri.
Printed in the UK by
W&G Baird Ltd.

Contents

Foreword By Adele Parks 4

Introduction By Allison Potter 5

List Of Illustrators 7

1   Fishfingers And Peaches..9

2   Parmo In Trouble...14

3   The Mysterious Ball..21

4   The Boy Behind The Letterbox...28

5   Parmo's Parade...34

About This Book...40

Foreword

Hello! As a Teessider myself, I am thrilled to be an ambassador for Middlesbrough Reads. It's brilliant to have the opportunity to shout about the incredibly important work being done in the region through this campaign. Helping children and families discover the magic of stories, while also giving them the skills they need to read confidently, is vital.

I believe reading is a basic human right that ought to be available to everyone. Sadly, some people think reading is not for them, they might even think books are boring! They're wrong of course! It's usually just a matter of that person not having discovered the right sort of book for them *yet*. Trust me, reading is incredible! Particularly as fluent readers are given unimaginable opportunities, not only in terms of education and improved mental health but also through pure joy and entertainment. Why would anyone want to miss out on that? I want to see all children given equal choices and chances through reading. I want to see them being excited, involved and inspired by books!

That's why I was absolutely delighted to hear about the creation of *Parmo to the Rescue!* by Rachael Wong with the help of Middlesbrough children – such a clever way to get children to see themselves as writers, as creators, as voices! I'm certain that not only did the creation of this book ease some boredom during lockdown but it will also have lit a lifelong passion for words, reading and books in many Middlesbrough children. I'm sure this book will become a firm favourite amongst families, in Middlesbrough and beyond.

Reading is a great way for families to spend time together and has so many benefits. It encourages children to be creative and use their imagination to picture the setting, the characters, and the story as it unfolds. It helps develop a sense of empathy which is important as they grow up and venture out into the world. Let's send out our Middlesbrough kids fully prepared, prepped and purposeful! We can do all that through gifting them a love of reading.

I want to say a massive CONGRATULATIONS to everyone involved in the creation of this book and give a huge CHEER to everyone who is holding it in their hands right now, because by buying, reading and noticing this book, you became part of the Middlesbrough Reads team.

Happy reading!
Love Adele Parks xxx
(Bestselling Author and Middlesbrough Reads Ambassador)

Introduction

I am thrilled that you are about to read *Parmo to the Rescue!* by the fantastic Rachael Wong and her co-authors – the children of Middlesbrough. Partly because it is a great story, but also because it captures why working in Middlesbrough is such an important part of the work of the National Literacy Trust. In your hand is an example of what can be done with brilliant authors, dedicated teachers, supportive partners and parents, and creative young people.

As a result of a longstanding partnership with Middlesbrough Football Club, when author (and Boro supporter) Rachael Wong wrote her book *The Bridge that George Built* for the MFC Foundation, Middlesbrough Reads was invited to meet with Rachael and invited to attend the book's launch at the Riverside Stadium.

In conjunction with Middlesbrough Council, the Marvellous Middlesbrough Writing Competition was launched and *The Bridge that George Built* was used as a stimulus, with a copy being sent to every school in the town. Fast-forward to the beginning of lockdown and, following consultation with Rachael, we developed the concept of 'a story in a week', written in partnership with the children of Middlesbrough via videos on the Middlesbrough Reads Facebook page.

Ideas and suggestions were posted each day, which Rachael cleverly included into the next chapter. The completed story was produced as an activity book for children to self-illustrate, coinciding with the launch of the illustration competition. Over 150 illustrations were submitted, long-listed and debated, with the successful ones being included in this version of the story.

The *Parmo to the Rescue!* project represents all the good things about Middlesbrough Reads – it provided an exciting opportunity for local children to work with an author, it was a way of recording a local story about the children of Middlesbrough's experience of lockdown and provided a fun literacy activity for the whole family to get involved with during challenging times.

Read, enjoy and share that enjoyment with others.

Allison Potter
(Middlesbrough Reads Literacy Hub Manager)

List Of Illustrators

Leighenna Adamson

Keironjames Boden

Amelia Carwardine

Emily Cook

Libby Dixon

Annabelle Drummond

Amelie Hammond

Hollie Jackson

Cole Landells

Jack Langsley

Owen Langsley

Eboni McGee

Kameron Moody

Jellisha Pracy Prabhu

Elexiss Reynolds

James Rumins

Naila Shafi

Scarlett Shaftoe

Amelia Shields

Ashton Shields

Evie Thirlway

Jessie Walker

Chelsea Whiteway

Mason Woolfall

Manahil Zakiuddin

Adam Zeib

Additional artwork by
Charlotte Potter and
Dominic Wong

Photo of Adele Parks courtesy of
Tom Banks *(banks-photo.co.uk)*

by Charlotte Potter

Dedicated to the children of Middlesbrough

All royalties from the sale of this book will be donated to Middlesbrough Reads.

by Amelia S

by Libby

1

Fishfingers And Peaches

"George! Leila! It's a quarter to eight," Dad called up the stairs. "Make sure you're down in ten minutes. You know how twitchy Mrs Jenkins gets if we're not all out the front in plenty of time for the NHS clap."

"OK," shouted Leila.

"Down in a minute," called George. He was in the middle of a game on his phone and was desperate to get to the next level before they had to go outside.

Normally, George didn't spend much time on his phone. Normally, he was too busy playing football. Football was George's first love, but since the lockdown started he hadn't been able to play much. Obviously, there were no training sessions or matches. Everyone had to keep apart so George couldn't even mess around with his mates, kicking a ball in the park or the playground. This made George feel sad. "Not doing sport makes me feel alone. It's an empty part of me," he had told Dad earlier.

by Jellisha

"I know it's hard," agreed Dad. "But we have to stay at home and take care, to keep people like Grandad safe."

George, his twin sister Leila, and Dad all lived with Grandad. Grandad was over 70 now so had to stay at home to avoid getting the virus that was causing the lockdown.

"Karim's in the same boat as you," Dad continued. "Mrs Khan has bad asthma so she's vulnerable too and needs protecting from the virus." Karim was one of George's best friends and only lived next door, but the boys couldn't play together. They weren't even allowed to kick a football over the fence to each other. The first reason for this was that the gardens in the street were very small. One poor kick and Mrs Underwood's greenhouse would be broken (again!). The second reason was Mrs Khan had declared that footballs spread infection. There was no point arguing when Mrs Khan made a pronouncement. Football over the fence was banned and that was the end of it. George realised he

9

was luckier than many children as Leila was a really good goalkeeper, but the garden was too small for the two of them to play a decent game, or even practise penalties, without the ball going into another garden all the time.

George and Karim played games online with each other. Occasionally, they talked on a video call, supposedly about schoolwork but the conversation always drifted onto guessing when football would start up again.

Both George and Leila were missing seeing their classmates in school and being able to chat about their schoolwork while they were doing it, working alongside each other. Although George and Leila were twins, and therefore in the same school year, there didn't seem to be much cooperation on schoolwork, or indeed on anything!

Part of the problem was the family only had one computer, so everyone was fighting to use it. In the mornings, George and Leila couldn't even agree whether to do Maths or English first. George liked to start the day with some Maths; Leila was adamant she wanted to do English. They bickered all day long knowing they shouldn't, and that it drove Grandad and Dad

by Chelsea

mad, but the twins were so frustrated to be stuck indoors they couldn't help themselves.

While Dad was at work, Grandad supervised home school and cooked the meals. The twins were too polite to say so, but they didn't think he was much good at either of these jobs. The answer to all their schoolwork questions was, "I'm not sure, they didn't do it like that in my day."

As for Grandad's cooking; he was hopeless! The fish fingers Grandad had cooked for tea were so burnt they reminded George of the charcoal sticks they sometimes used in art lessons at school. The kitchen cupboards were emptying fast (the twins were always hungry and it was hard for Dad to get to the shops) so Grandad was forced to come up with some strange combinations using what they had left. With the fish fingers, for example, Grandad had served chips, and tinned peaches as a vegetable.

Dad worked in a food distribution warehouse, so he was an important 'key worker' and had to keep going to work. The children were worried about Dad catching the virus at work, but he told them everyone was being very careful and the boss had come up with rules for keeping apart in the warehouse.

"The person we should all be worried about is Lucy," Dad told the twins. Lucy

by Eboni

"So do I," agreed Lucy, "But today some people who have recovered from the virus were well enough to go home. They were very pleased and grateful, so that was nice."

Thinking of nurses and hospitals, George suddenly remembered he had to go downstairs and join in the NHS clap. He raced down the stairs and out the front door. Grandad, Dad and Leila were already out there; so was most of the street, huddled in their doorways. Mrs Jenkins ran a tight ship on a Thursday night and everyone knew to be out in plenty of time.

But where was Mrs Jenkins? Her doorway was empty. This was astonishing to George; Mrs Jenkins was normally the first one out and the last one back in.

was Dad's girlfriend and she was a nurse in the big hospital in town. Leila had been very upset when she had seen Lucy on a video call on Dad's phone. Lucy looked very, very tired and her face was covered in big red marks from all the safety equipment and the mask she had to wear at work. "Oh Lucy," wailed Leila, "Look at your face! Are you ill?"

"No, I'm not ill, Leila," Lucy replied. "I'm just tired. I have had to wear a mask for a long time today and it makes my face sore."

"I hate this crisis!" Leila continued wailing.

by Chelsea

"Can't believe Mrs Jenkins is going to miss the clap," someone across the street shouted.

"She's probably fallen asleep in front of the telly," someone replied.

"She'll wake up when she hears us all making a racket," added someone else.

Grandad was worried. "I hope Mrs Jenkins is OK. It would be very unlike her to miss this."

Suddenly, everyone was clapping. It was 8pm. Still no Mrs Jenkins. Leila had a pan and a wooden spoon; she was making a

terrible din. Karim was blowing a whistle loudly. Looking over the wall to next door, George suddenly noticed that Karim's mum, Mrs Khan, was soaking wet. She was drenched from head to toe, and drips of water were falling off her headscarf!

As the clapping died down, George called over to Karim "What happened to your mam? I thought the swimming baths were closed!"

Karim gave George one of his cheeky grins. "The washing machine broke again. She can't ask your grandad to come and fix it like he usually does, so she's been watching videos on YouTube and trying to fix it herself. I think she must have had the phone upside down and pulled out the wrong pipe!"

While George and Karim had been talking over the wall, Grandad had been ringing Mrs Jenkins from his mobile to check on her. No one in the street had gone indoors; everyone was waiting to hear the news about Mrs Jenkins.

"You'd better get over there, Dan," said Grandad eventually to Dad, ending the call. "She's not very well and wants you to pop down and have a word, at a distance. Oh, and she says to wear some gloves please, she needs you to bring something back."

Word spread down the street, from doorstep to doorstep, like a forest fire on a hot day. "She's not very well – Dan's going to check on her…"

Dad looked alarmed. "She's not that ill," Grandad assured him. "She's just very tired and weak, and didn't want everyone seeing her in her dressing gown."

Dad set off. The whole street watched and waited. Various people called out messages as he went past, sending their best wishes, offering to do shopping for Mrs Jenkins, or cook her a meal.

Dad was at Mrs Jenkins' front door for a few minutes. No one could see Mrs Jenkins, she was too far back in her hallway. When Dad returned up the street he was carrying a crate with a basket inside, and a big bag of dog food. Beside Dad, on a lead, strutted Mrs Jenkins' cheeky little sausage dog called Parmo.

"Parmo!" shrieked George and Leila in delight.

by Naila

2

Parmo In Trouble

"Oh no, we're not having the dog are we?" asked Grandad as Dad came up the path with Parmo and all his clobber.

"Yes! Yes!" squealed Leila in delight. "We love Parmo!"

"Isn't Mrs Jenkins always telling us how naughty he is and that he chews everything?" continued Grandad. "I'm not sure about this Dan."

"It's OK Dad, it's just for a couple of nights until Mrs Jenkins is feeling better. It'll be a good distraction for the kids."

by Emily

by Jellisha

Grandad followed Dad into the house, still mumbling, but he had stopped actively protesting. George and Leila could smell victory. They sped into the house to welcome Parmo properly.

Parmo's arrival meant that George and Leila were late to bed that night. The little sausage dog had been very excited when he arrived and ran around downstairs, sniffing everything, barking

14

loudly, and chewing Grandad's shoes.

"Is this a dog or a small goat?" asked Grandad as he took his shoe from Parmo for the third time. "Thank goodness Mrs Jenkins has trained him not to go upstairs."

by Leighenna

"Come on, let's get you two into bed," Dad said to George and Leila eventually. "I've got an early start in the morning so I'll come up with you." As Dad went up the stairs, he called back to Grandad, "Could you pop Parmo in his crate for us please?"

Grandad looked at Parmo. Parmo looked back at Grandad. "I'm watching you," Grandad announced, as he lifted Parmo into his crate and followed the others upstairs.

The next morning, the scene of devastation in the front room was total. Dad had gone out to work very early and had come down the stairs and gone straight out of the front door, missing Parmo's trail of destruction.

Parmo had scratched the wallpaper, chewed the skirting boards, the cushions, Leila's goalkeeping gloves and George's football boots. The twins' footballs were looking deflated. Parmo had even chewed the laptop cable. Worst of all, Parmo had obviously rolled on a plastic bottle of ketchup someone had left on the coffee table. The rolling must have caused the lid to flip off and squirt ketchup all over the carpet.

When Grandad, George and Leila came down at eight o'clock, they were horrified. Clearly, Grandad hadn't shut the door to Parmo's crate properly. Parmo, exhausted by his efforts, was now fast asleep in his basket. Grandad sighed, "How could I be so daft not to close the door properly? Just look at the place! I didn't even take

by Leighenna

by Chelsea

15

by Hollie

by Ashton

my slippers up last night – they've been Parmo'd like everything else. Come on, let's have some breakfast before we clear this lot up."

"What about the laptop cable?" cried Leila. "What if the laptop doesn't work any more? How will we do our schoolwork?"

Grandad put his slippers on and inspected the damage to the cable. "He's not gone right through luckily. I'll tape it up today and hopefully your dad can find another one. He's a pest, that dog. Just look at my slippers?" said Grandad forlornly as he looked down at his toes poking out of the holes Parmo had chewed in the slippers.

"What about my football boots?" answered George. "If I can't find any new laces, I might have to train in my wellies!"

"Right," said Grandad after breakfast and the clearing up had been done. "What's the plan for school work today? It's Friday; don't they give you a project on Fridays?"

"Yes," answered Leila, logging on to the laptop and scowling at the taped up cable. "Here we are: a bit of English, a bit of Maths and then a creative project. The project can be anything at all to do with Middlesbrough or the virus. The best ones are going to be included in the assembly video next week. Oh no, it also says here we have to do the English and Maths first."

"You mean the Maths and the English?" started George.

"Now then, you two, I've had enough of that argument this week," interrupted Grandad. "Look, you can do today's English on some paper Leila, while George uses the laptop for the Maths. Then you can swap over when we have a morning break."

by Elexiss

by Evie

Leila scowled again. George seized the laptop triumphantly.

"So, what are you going to do for your project?" George asked Leila when they stopped for a morning break of a drink and a biscuit.

"Easy peasy, I'm going to do a dance routine with my friends, warning people about having to wash their hands and staying at home. We'll all record it separately and then put it all together just like they do on TV. In fact, I'm going to go and message Olivia and Martha now to tell them what we're doing."

Leila bounded up the stairs to find her phone. "Make sure you're back in five minutes to do your Maths," Grandad shouted after her. He then turned to George, "What about you then George? Any ideas for your project?"

"Not sure, Grandad. Something to do with football, obviously. I like making stuff and junk modelling too. It's a shame I can't do it with Karim. It would be much more fun than doing it on my own."

"Well, I could help you with it?" offered Grandad. "Let's get my box of Boro treasures out and see what ideas it gives us."

'Oh no,' thought George. 'I'll be stuck for hours listening to all Grandad's old stories about Boro and looking at all that dusty stuff in his box.' His heart sank. "Thanks Grandad, that would be great. Just let me finish my English first."

Dad's shift finished at lunchtime. He came home and took Parmo for a walk. George went with him, mainly to avoid all the squealing from Leila and her friends, who were planning their dance routine on a video call. The problem seemed to be that some of the girls did ballet, but the others did street dance, and no one could agree on a routine. "I know," suggested Leila, "we'll do a mash up, you know, Sugar Plum Fairy with somersaults, flips and cartwheels. Then we'll finish up with some flossing and some freestyle football skills....."

George fled out the door at this point. He had heard enough!

"I miss football," confided George to Dad, as they walked Parmo. "I miss playing, training, kicking about with my mates, taking penalties in the park with Leila, watching Boro. I miss all of it."

"So do I," agreed Dad. "And Grandad does too. I was thinking about that project you have to do. Let's involve Grandad. Let him help you with a Boro project. He would really enjoy that."

George had no choice. By the time he and Dad got home, Grandad had already brought his box of Boro treasures downstairs and was unpacking it. "Grandad, shall we do the Boro project together?" George asked. "You know how Boro used to play at Ayresome Park before they moved to the Riverside? I thought perhaps we could make a model of Ayresome Park and the streets around it, even the ice cream shop you always tell me about. We could use cereal packets and stuff."

Grandad was beaming with joy. "Great idea, George. You know Ayresome Park was a World Cup venue? I saw three World Cup matches there in 1966, including North Korea beating Italy, which was a major upset at the time. As kids, we loved the North Korean team in that World Cup. They played their matches at Ayresome Park, wore red shirts like Boro and they brought no supporters of their own so we adopted them. Here, I've still got the match programmes in this box, they'll be worth a bob or two. Hold on a minute, there's only two of them here. Where on earth is the other one...?"

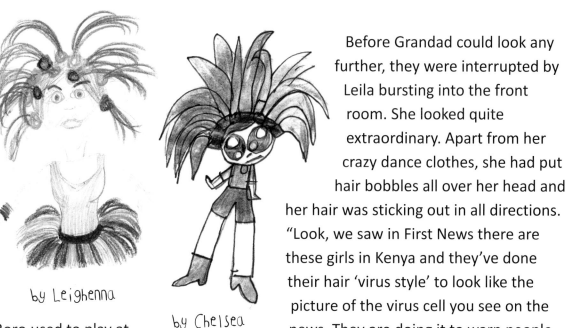

by Leighenna

by Chelsea

by Amelie

Before Grandad could look any further, they were interrupted by Leila bursting into the front room. She looked quite extraordinary. Apart from her crazy dance clothes, she had put hair bobbles all over her head and her hair was sticking out in all directions. "Look, we saw in First News there are these girls in Kenya and they've done their hair 'virus style' to look like the picture of the virus cell you see on the news. They are doing it to warn people to keep apart and not spread the virus."

"Well, nobody's going to go near you, looking like that," offered George.

Leila ignored him and carried on. "We're going to give the same message with a mixture of a dance routine and freestyle football. We just need a cool name now."

"Lockdown Leila and The Germ Girls?" suggested George. Dad was trying not to laugh. To keep the peace he said to George, "Talking of freestyle football, haven't you got some football drills that new coach Carlin sent you and Leila to do

19

by Amelie

knew Parmo would start interfering otherwise. The drills involved dribbling through cones (George only had three cones so he used some baked bean cans as well), kick ups, drag backs, rainbow flicks and step overs. George really had to concentrate to control the ball properly in such a small space.

After a while, George looked up and realised he couldn't hear Parmo making a noise any more. Parmo's ball was lying on the ground, but there was no sign of Parmo. The back door was still closed, so Parmo hadn't gone indoors. Heading towards the back gate, George looked in horror at the freshly dug hole under the fence. Parmo had dug a hole out of the garden and into the alley at the back of the house.

by Leighenna

while training's off? Why don't you go out the back to practise your drills and I'll watch the first part of Leila's routine? Take Parmo with you please; that smell is terrible. Mrs Jenkins did warn me that if we let him scavenge food off the floor then we would regret it later!"

George was about to protest, but then he remembered it was his fault Parmo had been scavenging food off the floor. He had spilled cereal at breakfast time, dropped peas at teatime and a crisp in the afternoon. Parmo had hoovered it all up. "Come on Parmo, let's go."

Dad had printed out the drills from Carlin so George put them on the ground and started working through them. He gave Parmo another ball to keep him occupied as George

The Mysterious Ball

Quickly, George unlocked the gate and ran out into the alley behind the house. Parmo was not in the alley. George could see the usual army of bins, standing to attention like sentries next to each back gate. Mrs Hanratty was just putting a bag in her bin, while one of her cats wound itself around her legs affectionately. She nodded to George and went back through her gate with the cat. George didn't like being out in the alley at the best of times. There was a strange echo and the alley felt dirty and uncared for. There was rubbish and broken glass on the ground, plus the bins smelt disgusting. Even the pink and yellow flowers in the hanging basket by Mrs Underwood's gate looked a bit wilted and unloved. George didn't like the cobblestones either. When he was younger he had twisted his ankle badly on the uneven surface while he and Karim were playing tag.

Slowly, George walked along the alley, searching between bins, peeping over fences, avoiding the stinging nettles, trying to find any trace of Parmo. There was a motorbike at the end of the alley that belonged to Dave the chef. The bike seemed to spend most of its time in pieces, surrounded by tools.

George knew he shouldn't really be out in the alley during lockdown and so, feeling helpless, he turned back towards home to tell everyone that Parmo was missing.

Just as he reached his back gate, George heard some muffled barking behind him. He turned round and there was Parmo, wagging his tail, long silky ears bouncing up and down, eyes

by Jellisha

gleaming with the excitement of a dog with a prize. Parmo did indeed have a prize. The reason for his muffled barking was plain to see – his mouth was completely filled with a tennis ball.

George gave Parmo a stroke. "You're a naughty dog. Digging tunnels like that! What have you got here?" There was some writing on the tennis ball but George couldn't read it properly. For a start it wasn't written very neatly, and

by James

by Jessie

secondly, George suspected most of the writing was currently in Parmo's mouth. George could just about make out the letters 'HE'. Perhaps the ball belonged to someone called Henry?

by Mason

by Annabelle

George tried to take the ball out of Parmo's mouth to have a better look. Parmo was happy to let go as he assumed George would then throw the ball for him to fetch. The dog was disappointed when George turned the ball over in his hand and showed no signs of being about to throw it. George was astonished to see the full message on the ball. It didn't say 'HENRY'; it said 'HELP'!

George wasn't at all sure what to do now. Had the message been written today, or was it weeks or even months old? Was it part of a game, or did someone really need help? Even if someone was in need of help, George had no idea where Parmo had found the ball. Sadly, Parmo couldn't tell George where he had found the ball (although he was currently doing a very good job of telling George he wanted him to throw the ball!).

"Not now Parmo, give over. Come on inside, we need to have a think about this ball."

George decided he needed a bit of help deciding what to do about the mysterious message on the ball. He opened the back door and stepped into the kitchen. Grandad was standing in the middle of the kitchen looking stressed, surrounded by a huge mountain of pots, pans, dishes, packets, vegetables and cooking utensils.

by keironjames

George suspected that every item in the kitchen drawers and cupboards was now out on the surface.

"Clear off you, and take that dog with you," called Grandad in a cheerful voice. "I'm having a cooking lesson from Rosie – you can say hello – she's teaching me how to make lasagne."

George waved at Grandad's phone, which was propped up on the kettle. There was Grandad's friend Rosie, looking relaxed with a cup of tea in a very tidy kitchen.

by Leighenna

Grandad.

She waved back at George and winked. George understood. He also knew he couldn't interrupt Rosie's lasagne masterclass with a half baked story about a funny old tennis ball. Especially as George was very much looking forward to a properly cooked meal and didn't want to ruin his chances of getting one.

George and Parmo went through to the front room. Leila was in the middle of practising her routine with Olivia and Martha, who were on the laptop screen. Leila stopped when George came in. "Stop disturbing us, George," Leila complained. "We're in the middle of a tricky bit. We're just finishing the indoor part before we do our freestyle football skills. Go away!"

George had no desire to hang around with Leila and The Germ Girls, or whatever they were called. He closed the front room door and sat on the bottom step of the stairs. Dad would be having a nap upstairs after his early shift. Who could George talk to about the ball?

"Karim will know," thought George with certainty. The ball might even be one of Karim's and that would solve the mystery immediately. George took out his phone and called Karim on a video call, as he wanted Karim to be able to see the ball.

"Alright?" Karim answered. "Fancy a game of FIFA? Or am I too good for you? I don't mind playing Minecraft or Rocket

24

by Leighenna

"Someone needing help?" giggled George. Then he added, "Seriously, though, do you think someone wrote that today, or ages ago?"

"Difficult to tell," replied Karim, "it's been in Parmo's mouth for a start. I tell you what, let's try and work out who could have written it. It's definitely not Mr or Mrs Underwood, on the other side of us. Mum was only talking to Mrs Underwood this morning while they were both hanging their washing out. On our side of the alley, then, that leaves the Dovers…"

"Ugh," interrupted George, "Those teenage girls are awful, always arguing. They think they're so cool talking in slang all the time but no one can understand a word they say. I've heard them today so they're fine. Not sure I'd want to help them anyway!"

"Then there's Mrs Bunning…"

"She left cupcakes for Grandad this morning…"

"And Steven."

"Ah, I saw him out the window getting into his car today. Dad says he's helping to give out food at a foodbank as he can't go to any schools at the moment."

by Adam

League if that'll give you more of a chance!"

"Yeah, suppose so. Just need to wait until Leila's out of the front room. Guess what? Parmo just escaped out into the alley and came back with this ball." George held up the ball for Karim to see. "Is it yours?"

Karim looked closely. "Nah, not mine. Help? Who writes 'Help' on a ball?"

Steven worked for Middlesbrough FC Foundation and had been into George and Karim's school talking to them about going up to secondary school. The boys thought Steven was

by Ashton

25

great because he had a job where you could wear a cool tracksuit to work.

"What about the other side of the alley?" asked Karim. "Who do we know on that side?"

"Well, there's Mrs Burnett, the nice teacher lady. Remember when we saw her getting into her car dressed as a blue pencil on World Book Day?"

Karim laughed. "Yeah, that was funny. I saw her sitting in her garden earlier when I looked out the window."

"Next to her is that annoying Marcus kid. Grandad always moans when he and his dad go to watch Boro – he says you can bank on it being a 0-0 draw if they go. Don't think the ball's from them."

"Yes, his dad's cutting the grass again, I can see him from up here," Karim agreed before adding, "Mam reckons he finishes the lawn off with scissors to make it perfect, but I've never seen him do it."

"And it can't be Mrs Hanratty because she was putting a bag in the bin when I was out in the alley. I don't think it's Dave the chef either as it looked like he'd been working on the bike when I went out there."

by Cole

"So," summarized Karim "it has to be one of the houses that back onto the other side of the alley. Either the end one or the one three doors down...."

"I don't like the sound of all this plotting," announced a loud voice in the background. "What are you boys up to?" Half of Mrs Khan's head appeared in the screen, making George jump with surprise. Why did grown-ups always have to talk so loudly on the phone?

Karim started to explain about the ball. Mrs Khan had only heard half of the story when she threw up her hands in horror. "You mean someone has cried for help and you two boys are treating it like a puzzle? George, go and wake your dad straight away. Tell him what's happened. With my asthma, I can't go out, but he can go and take a look."

"OK, Mrs Khan," said George meekly. "I'll go and do that. Call you later, Karim."

George ended the call and started up the stairs. He hadn't got more than halfway up when Dad appeared, looking very sleepy. "Sorry Dad, I didn't mean to wake you...."

"It was double Mrs Khan that woke me," laughed Dad. "I could hear her up the stairs – and through the window!

by Jack

What's got her in such a state?"

George explained to Dad what had happened and how he and Karim had worked out which houses the ball might have come from. Dad considered for a short while. "Well, it's probably nothing to worry about, but Mrs Khan could be right and someone might need our help. These are strange times and it's worth checking out. Come on, let's go and take a look round the neighbourhood."

"But Dad, we've already been out once today, with Parmo, and we're only supposed to go out once."

"Exceptional circumstances," Dad winked. "Besides, Mrs Jenkins is the only one who would comment and she's ill in bed!"

by Jellisha

The Boy Behind The Letterbox

George and Dad set out to investigate where the mystery ball had come from, and if there was indeed someone in the neighbourhood who needed help. They took Parmo with them. Grandad was glad of an excuse to get Parmo out of the way while he was having his cooking lesson.

It was late afternoon. Normally, the street would be busy with cars and people returning from work or school. Now, it was eerily quiet. Apart from a lady with red hair walking a greyhound at the other end of the street, the only movement was a lone purple chocolate wrapper blowing down the

by Hollie

by Jellisha

middle of the road between the parked cars. Parmo stopped and pulled on the lead, giving serious consideration to chasing the greyhound. "Forget it mate," laughed Dad, "You're a sausage dog with short little legs, there's no point chasing greyhounds – they were designed for running!"

"Do you know what I think about the ball," said George as they walked along. "I think one of the Boro footballers might live in the next street and he hurt himself doing keepie uppies so he had to throw the ball to get help because he's injured on the floor."

"Nice idea, George, but don't you think we would know if a Boro footballer lived on the next street?" laughed Dad. "For a start, Grandad would have found out from Mrs Jenkins and then Grandad would've been on the footballer's doorstep every Monday morning telling him how he needs to get forward more, keep hold of the ball, and tackle properly."

"Yes, that's true," admitted George.

"Come on," said Dad encouragingly, "Let's take a look at those two houses on the next street that you and Karim thought we should check out."

As George and Dad turned the corner at the end of their street, they saw Roberto, the friendly Brazilian man who ran the crazy golf course in the park. As he got closer, they could see that Roberto was wearing an eye patch. "Crikey man, what happened to you?" asked Dad as they drew level.

"You won't believe it," replied Roberto, "but on the very last day before lockdown some kid hit a golf ball onto the windmill on hole 9. It bounced off one of the sails, straight through the ticket office window, and hit me in the eye. No permanent damage luckily, but I've got to wear this for a while. I feel like a pirate! Anyway, I must go and get in the queue at the chemists for my eyedrops."

Dad was still shaking his head in disbelief when they turned into the next street. "This one, on the corner," George said, tugging Dad's sleeve. They went through the small gate to ring the doorbell and immediately could see a bag of shopping on the doorstep.

Dad frowned, "That's a bit odd." He rang the doorbell and a few moments later it was opened by a tiny old lady with dark curly hair and a friendly face. Behind her, George could see a big dresser in the passageway, full of plates and vases, some with flowers in. Next to the dresser, on a small table, was an old fashioned telephone with holes for your fingers. George had always wanted to have a go on one of them.

Before Dad could say anything to the old lady, she saw the shopping on the doorstep and exclaimed, "Oh dear, I forgot to bring the shopping in. Mrs Hanratty got me some bits earlier. She did message me to say they were there but I forgot to bring them in. Anyway, how can I help you? That's a very sweet little sausage dog you have there."

"Believe me, he's not sweet, he's a menace most of the time," said Dad. "We live in the next street and Parmo here found a tennis ball with the word 'Help' written on it. We were just checking everyone's OK."

"That's very good of you," smiled the old lady, "but I'm fine. Just a bit lonely, you know how it is. All my children have grown up and live a long way away, but Mrs Hanratty has been good getting my shopping for me. I'm Josie, by the way." Josie saw George looking at the old telephone in the hall. "It does work, you know," she laughed, "so, if I did need help I could phone someone. I wouldn't need to write on a tennis ball. I doubt I could throw one very far anyway! After the lockdown, perhaps you would like to come round and have a go, young man? What's your name?"

"I'm George," answered George politely.

"And I'm...." started Dad, "Oh no...Parmo!" Whilst everyone had been talking, Parmo had sneakily popped his head into the shopping bag and pulled out a packet of ham, which he

by Jellisha

was now busy trying to open with his teeth. "Oh Josie, I'm very sorry," apologised Dad. "I'll bring you some more ham tomorrow. Parmo, you're a menace!"

"Don't worry," Josie laughed, "I shouldn't have left the shopping out. It was very nice to meet you though and hopefully I will see you again George."

Dad and George stepped back out into the street. Dad had Parmo's lead in one hand and the incriminating mangled packet of ham in the other.

"Let's quickly try the house three doors down now," suggested Dad. "I think we should aim to get home before Parmo causes any more trouble."

George was not impressed when they reached the house. The front gate was broken and the small garden was full of broken slabs and weeds. Paint on the front door was peeling away and one of the panes of glass at the top of the door was broken. Someone had hung a dirty blanket across the inside of the front window. All George could see was the bottom half of an action man poking through the blanket on the windowsill. "Mrs Khan would have words to say about this house," George whispered to Dad.

"Don't judge people until you know more about them," Dad replied. "There could be a very good reason why the person or people in this house can't look after it very well."

by Owen

The house didn't have a doorbell, so Dad knocked gently on the door. There was no answer. Dad knocked again, a little more loudly. George thought he could hear a faint movement behind the door, but perhaps he had imagined it because still no one answered the door.

George and Dad looked at each other, uncertain what to do. George was a little scared in front of this strange house, but it helped knowing Dad was there too.

Suddenly, Parmo ran forward, his nose right up to the door, and started barking. "Parmo, behave," Dad warned Parmo in an irritated voice. "You've caused enough trouble. Come on George, there's no one here. Let's go home and decide what to do next."

Dad pulled on Parmo's lead, but Parmo really didn't want to come and just kept barking at the door. In a sudden moment of bravery, George stepped forward, opened the letterbox and looked through. To George's astonishment there was a pair of small blue eyes looking through from the other side of the letterbox. The eyes had a little voice and the little voice said, "Is that the sausage dog? I'm hungry. All the biscuits are finished and Mammy is too ill to go and get any more. I threw the ball when I saw the dog because I want someone to bring some more biscuits."

by Ashton

"George, George, is there someone there?" Dad had grabbed George's shoulder. "What are they saying?"

"It's a little boy. He says he threw the ball because his mam is ill and they've run out of biscuits."

Dad looked concerned. George felt he could almost see wheels turning inside Dad's head, working out what to do. "Ask him his name?"

George relayed the question through the door.

"Tommy," the little boy replied.

"How old are you Tommy?"

"I'm six."

"He's Tommy and he's six. Do you want me to ask him if he knows how to open the door?"

"No," replied Dad firmly. "I want you to keep talking to him while I ring the police."

George's eyes widened in alarm. "Don't worry," Dad reassured him, "Nobody's in trouble, but the police will have people specially trained to deal with situations like this and they'll make sure Tommy is properly looked after."

The next hour or so was a bit of a blur to George. First, a police car arrived, then an ambulance, and some people went into the house. Neighbours started coming out of their houses to see what was going on. Dad spent a lot of time talking to a police officer, explaining to her what had happened. George was left with Parmo on the street. He tickled Parmo's ears and told him he was a clever dog for finding the little boy. When Dad wasn't looking, George opened the packet of ham and Parmo ate it all!

Soon after, the police officer came over to George to tell him that Tommy's mum was ill and needed to go to hospital, but she would be fine and Tommy would be well looked after too. The officer said George and Parmo had done very well, but it was time for them to go home now.

"Can I wave to Tommy first?" George asked.

"Yes of course you can," replied the officer. George waved to the little boy, huddled in a blanket next to another police officer, just inside the house. He was drinking from a bottle of water and eating a bar of chocolate.

"Come on," said Dad. "Let's get home. Grandad will be disappointed if we miss his lasagne."

In all the drama, George had completely forgotten about Grandad's lasagne. George was starving. He hoped Grandad's lasagne was a big one!

5

Parmo's Parade

Looking back, nearly a week later, Grandad's lasagne seemed like a turning point in the lives of the Jones family. The lasagne was a triumph and Grandad was so proud of his efforts he decided to have a cooking lesson from Rosie every day. Luckily, Dad did a big shop at the weekend. It was also lucky that Rosie had nothing better to do with her time!

"Well, our teachers did say we should learn something new during lockdown," Leila teased Grandad at teatime the following Thursday night. "I am sure they meant grandads too."

"Lots of people are learning new stuff," agreed George. "Look at Mrs Khan. She's not just fixed her washing machine, she's made Karim set her up with her own YouTube channel giving advice on fixing washing machines, how to wash clothes on the best programme and what products to use if you can't get hold of your usual ones in lockdown. Karim can't believe it – she's got loads of subscribers. She's a YouTube sensation!"

"Ah, but is she as much of a sensation as Lockdown Leila and The Germ Girls?" laughed Leila.

George was very amused that Leila and her friends had stuck with the joke name he had given them. In fact, George

by Jellisha

by Jellisha

by Leighenna

by Emily

had even appeared briefly in the video, doing some freestyle football tricks alongside Leila in the garden. Dad had sent the video to Lucy, and Lucy loved it so much she had shown it to her patients at the hospital. They loved it too, so Lockdown Leila and The Germ Girls had a fan club at the hospital now. Lucy said the video had lifted everyone's spirits and she had even seen some of the other nurses doing part of the dance routine in the corridor.

One of the patients told the local radio station about the dance video in the hospital that had cheered the patients up. The next thing, Leila was on the radio telling everyone about it! BBC Tees was doing a special 'feel good festival' programme about all the amazing acts of kindness happening in Teesside during lockdown. As it was a special all day show, with two presenters in separate studios, Leila was delighted to get to speak with both her favourite presenters – Gary Philipson and Antony Collins.

Leila was equally pleased that Lockdown Leila and The Germ Girls featured in the weekly assembly video, which had arrived in their inbox that morning. George and Grandad's model of Ayresome Park also appeared in the assembly video, but not in quite the way anyone had intended. Grandad was even more proud of their appearance than George was, although he was slightly annoyed that Parmo had (once again!) stolen the show. The model had taken George and Grandad a few evenings to construct, mainly because Grandad kept stopping to refer to old newspaper articles from

by Manahil

by Chelsea

his treasure box to make sure the model was 100% accurate. While Grandad was checking the articles, George had to keep Parmo from chewing the cereal packets, rolling around with the sellotape and trying to play football with the glue stick. Dad said it was so funny he took some video of Ayresome Park being Parmo'd. Everyone agreed the video was hilarious so George sent it in with his finished photo and it all appeared in the online assembly.

Grandad was the only one who found the project stressful. "If that dog destroys Ayresome Park, after all our hard work, I'll...."

"You'll do what?" asked Dad. "Be careful what you say. The dog's a hero now."

"Yes, Parmo's a hero," agreed Leila. "Everyone's saying it. Parmo found the ball and then helped rescue Tommy and his mam."

It was true; Parmo was now something of a local celebrity. George had enjoyed taking Parmo for walks this week. Everyone they met shouted over to them what a clever pair they were. Mr Underwood even called out, "Look out, it's Batman and Robin."

"Yeah, right," Leila said when George told her at teatime. "Parmo's Batman and you're Robin."

Dad saw another argument brewing so he quickly interrupted. "I had a call earlier to say that Tommy's mam is recovering well in hospital. Tommy is staying with his auntie in Darlington but he and his mam should be home soon."

"Perhaps after lockdown we could go and see Tommy?" suggested George.

"Oh yes," Dad replied. "In fact I think a few of us are planning to go round and help tidy the place up as soon as we are able to. Mrs Underwood has her eye on the garden. I can give the front door a lick of paint and Tony up the road can replace the glass in the door. We'll get Steven to sort them a food box."

"Perhaps I could make them one of my delicious cakes?" offered Grandad.

"Only if you make one for us too!" both twins said at once.

"Well, that one over there is for Mrs Jenkins. Your dad is going to take it round to her tonight when he takes Parmo home – finally! In fact, you two might have to go and help him; he'll have the dog and all its gear as well as the cake."

"Oh, I can't believe Parmo's going home...." Leila started to wail.

Grandad stopped her in her tracks. "Well, Mrs Jenkins is a lot better now and she's missing Parmo. We should be pleased for her that she's better. Besides, she knows how much you love Parmo and she's said you can take him for a walk any time you like. Plus Parmo can come for sleepovers at the weekend when things get more normal. Preferably on my darts night," added Grandad with a nod over to the place on the kitchen floor where Parmo usually sat during meal times. It was the perfect position to see anything that was dropped from the table – accidentally or on purpose. Parmo wasn't in his usual spot, though. "Where is that dog, anyway? Causing trouble, I expect. It's suspiciously quiet everywhere."

by Chelsea

Grandad got up from the table and went into the front room. After a while, the twins and Dad heard Grandad exclaim, "Well I never. Fancy that!" They all rushed into the front room to find Grandad and Parmo on the floor behind the settee.

"What's going on, Grandad? Are you OK?"

"I'm delighted. That's what I am," replied Grandad.

He emerged slowly from behind the settee clutching his missing Ayresome Park 1966 World Cup programme. "Well I never," he repeated. "Parmo's found my lost programme right down the back of the settee. And look, he hasn't even chewed it yet; I got to him just in time. It must have fallen out of the box when I had it down at Christmas. What a coincidence: when the World Cup trophy was stolen in 1966 it was found by Pickles the dog. Now my 1966 World Cup programme has been found by a dog called Parmo."

"Oooh, well done Parmo, you clever boy." Leila gave Parmo a big cuddle. "It's Parmo to the rescue again!"

"Come on," said Dad. "Let's finish our tea. It'll soon be time for the NHS clap. Parmo's going home straight afterwards; so we'll need some time to get all his stuff ready. Mrs Jenkins is up and about and on patrol now, we mustn't be late."

Normal service had indeed been resumed. When the Jones family came out of their front door at five minutes to eight, Mrs Jenkins was already on her doorstep, surveying the street; like royalty but without the balcony. The rest of the

street joined them. Mrs Khan was looking very glamorous. She had obviously come straight from filming!

After the clap for the NHS, no one went back indoors. Everyone stayed out to give an equally big clap (and a few cheers) as Parmo the Hero was returned ceremoniously to Mrs Jenkins. Parmo was at the head of a procession involving George, Leila, a crate, a basket, the cake, some tins of dog food, and Dad. Life on the street was starting to return to normal; Parmo was going home.

Grandad stood in his doorway and watched this strange procession for a while, smiling at how families, friends and neighbours had come together (at a distance). "Parmo to the rescue indeed!" he chuckled to himself, and then he went inside.

The End

by kameron

About This Book

About the National Literacy Trust

Our charity is dedicated to improving the reading, writing, speaking and listening skills of those who need it most, giving them the best possible chance of success in school, work and life. We run Literacy Hubs and campaigns in communities where low levels of literacy and social mobility are seriously impacting people's lives. We support schools and early years settings to deliver outstanding literacy provision, and we campaign to make literacy a priority for politicians, businesses and parents. Our research and analysis make us the leading authority on literacy and drive our interventions. Literacy is a vital element of action against poverty and our work changes children's life stories.

Visit literacytrust.org.uk to find out more, donate or sign up for our free email newsletter. You can also find us on Facebook, Twitter and Instagram.

The National Literacy Trust is a registered charity no. 1116260 and a company limited by guarantee no. 5836486 registered in England and Wales and a registered charity in Scotland no. SC042944. Registered address: 68 South Lambeth Road, London SW8 1RL.

About Middlesbrough Reads

The National Literacy Trust Hub in Middlesbrough, known locally as Middlesbrough Reads, works in partnership with Middlesbrough Council and the Middlesbrough Promise to forge links in the local community and improve literacy in Middlesbrough.

⊙ middlesbroughreads.org.uk

f Middlesbrough Reads Facebook

🐦 #BoroReads